THE LAST STRAW

Author: JaunKerra Sanders

Illustrator: Thaddeus Wilkins

Chapter 1

A new school, a new life once again, thought Denise White as she entered North Bay High school, a school not similar at all to the last four schools she had attended in the past year and a half. Living with an oh-so-sweet, ignore the drama mom and a high tempered step father who could snap at any minute had to be the worst! Her mom had constantly told her that she should always be grateful because there was always someone with a life one hundred times worse than your own. That's just a bunch of crap, she thought. If I ever found that person I would give them a million dollars and be a slave to them the rest of my life.

The second she had that thought, she wanted to take it back. Getting pushed against a locker was a fat, ugly, dark-skinned kid, who looked like he wasn't having a good first day of school at all. She put her headphones in and proceeded to listen to Beyonce's LEMONADE album. She did not need to get involved with anything that wasn't her business.

****

"I don't have any money today, Eugene", Micheal Drake said, hoping he wouldn't get punched in the eye or nose and have his new glasses ruined. His mom would be really upset if she had to buy him a new pair. Last year he had a total of four new pairs of glasses. The first one he had lost and the last three had been broken by a bully having a bad day. Every time he had told his mom he had lost the previous pair she would curse him out and in a couple of days buy a new pair. She struggled being a single mother trying to raise him and his younger brother. Both of their fathers were drug dealers. Maybe he shouldn't even ask her for a new pair if these were ruined. It wasn't like the glasses helped his grades improve. Last year he had barely passed with one F and all Ds. His class rank was 125 out of 126. For a moment, he felt sorry for whoever was number 126, but then again, who cared? At least it wasn't him.

"I better have your lunch on my table gay boy, or you won't live to see tomorrow", Eugene said, giving him one final shove and walking away.

****

Eugene Norman Jr. (known by most of his family, friends, and victims as EJ) walked down the hallway looking for more losers to terrorize. I need some money and I aint goin say it no mo, he thought as heard someone clowning his favorite rapper Birdman. Birdman hadn't had a good hit in a minute but his songs were tough. Birdman was a GOAT and would forever be in his book.

Today was the first day of school, and he had to make it known to everyone, old and new, who he was and why he should be respected. In his world, some people—mainly fat, ugly, or weird people—were created to be someone's property. What else could be the purpose of their existence? They needed someone like him to be there to knock some sense in to them every day. He loved being that guy. He loved to see that terrified look in someone's eye when he turned a corner. It was like playing cat and mouse. He was the predator and they were prey. He could do or say whatever he wanted to them, and they wouldn't even whisper one word. They knew to put some respeck on his name! It was how he had always gotten a little extra money on the side or a little extra lunch on the table. The lunch he got from the little queer Drake today could be saved for his dinner tonight. His old man most likely wouldn't bring home any grub tonight, if he even decided to come home. Hopefully he won't come home, he thought. That way I can just hang with the guys tonight. He had the weed they would need to have a slow and easy night. All he needed was someone to get the car, bottles ,and hoes. As he turned the corner, he saw the right guy for the job.

****

"What up, EJ?," said Tremaine Webb, one of EJ's best friends and also one of the football team's most valued players.

"Nothing," replied EJ. "Trying to find something to get into tonight. You know…. celebrate being back in this old dump."

"Yeah, man. I don't know what I'm getting into after football practice, hopefully some chick's bed. You know the girls here now are so easy to get to."

"I know what you mean, man," EJ laughed, "But I just got some new stuff we need to try tonight.

You trying to get high? I got all we need except the drinks."

"Well I can get that, so I'll pick you up around seven. Maybe get some of these girls to come too."

"Alright, see you then," EJ replied and walked away.

How in the world am I going to get a few drinks out of the little black freezer? Tremaine thought to himself. His uncle would most likely be working the night shift, but how would he get past his aunt? She would take his car keys and beat the breaks off of him if he even thought about picking up a can of beer. He would just have to hope for the best. He was not going to be the one to spoil the evening. He refused to end his senior year without losing his virginity. He played like he was the man, but the thought of even touching a girl scared him; especially after what had happened to his mother. Yeah, tonight would be the night, he smiled as he closed his locker and walked to class.......

Chapter 2

A project already? Denise thought to herself as she grabbed some peaches and put them on her nearly empty lunch tray. Everything about this town and especially this school screamed poor, including the lunch. Even the teachers looked poor, and they all had an attitude problem. Why did teachers have to always ask for too much? Didn't they know that we have a life outside of school?

Well, she couldn't use that as an excuse at all considering the fact that she did nothing all day but read books. Still, she was just finishing up the last chapter of a new book—the chapter where the main character finds out that her husband is having an affair with his sister. She was going to finish last night, but it was 11:30 and she had to make sure she had her clothes and supplies ready for her first day of senior year at a new school. Everyone knew you always had to make a good first impression. She may still have time to read the book this afternoon if she did all her homework in a within a reasonable time frame.

As she sat down at an empty table, she heard a group of girls talking. One of the girls, she remembered, was in her Spanish class. She was a skinny, tall blonde that acted like a snob. When the teacher asked her tell the class her name and something about herself, she stood up, rolled her eyes and said,

"My name is Lisa and I hate when I'm talking and someone interrupts me. I'm a queen, and I deserve to be treated like one." Denise immediately knew she would never hang around someone like that even for a million dollars.

"Yeah they said the party at Lil Corey's house tonight 'pose to be lit," Lisa said. "No parents and all the guys from the football team goin' be there."

"Is Tremaine going to be there? You still haven't talked to him yet, have you?" asked the girl sitting next to her.

"Hell no, Tiya! I'm waiting for him to approach me. I never had to ask a guy out before, and I'm not about to start asking them out now."

"Ha! Well he can be the first guy you ask out and the last guy you let get into your panties," Tiya replied.

"Shut up! You act like I'm a hoe or something. If I do let him, he will only be the fifth."

"The fifth...really??? More like the eighth. May I remind you about Mike, Darrell, Christian, Shawn, Corey, Bryant, Trey....."

"Okay! Eighth....but who cares? You're just mad cause you can't get them like I can!"

I can't take it anymore, Denise thought as she got up from the table with her tray. That was the last time she would ever eavesdrop on a conversation. Now she knew her mother was also right about eavesdropping. You might hear something you didn't want or need to hear. She hated the way her mom was always right.

As she threw away her tray she tried to figure out how one girl could lay down with so many guys. Never lay down with dogs, or you'll get up with fleas—another one of her mom's sayings. Eight guys might be a little bit to some people, but it was a lot to her.....let's see.....zero!! Well there was that time when..... no, she wouldn't count that. She wouldn't even think about that right now.

When she opened the door to the two-stall, dirty, cramped bathroom, she heard someone crying. The sobs were coming from the second stall, where the door was wide open. She didn't want to be nosey, but it seemed as though the sobs where getting louder and louder. She went to the door and saw a short black girl sitting up against the wall with her head in her lap.

"What am I going to do?" she screamed to herself. "I'm trying to be brave and hang on, but I just can't do it anymore!"

Speechless, Denise stood in the doorway. "Hi, I'm Denise...are you okay? Can I help you with anything?"

"No,I'm fine! You wouldn't understand anyway. I saw you move in across the street. You have the perfect family don't you? I don't need your help! Just stay away from me, or there will be a problem, got it?"

"Whatever," Denise replied, rolling her eyes and walking to Pre Calc.

All through class she heard people talk about the party. Nobody even bothered to do the assignment Mrs. Smith had given, but then again, who really wanted to do math on the first day of school?

Almost everyone said they were going to the party except that poor kid named Michael- the kid she seen getting pushed against the locker. Denise finally found out his name and that he was picked on mostly because of his weight and the fact that he had never had a girlfriend. She felt sorry for him,but she had problems of her own. A part of her really wanted to go to the party tonight. The other part of her thought it was a bad idea. What was the point of going somewhere where you knew nobody and nobody knew you?

"Hey Ma!! What up? What's your name?"

Huh? Denise stared at the big-muscled, chocolate toned guy with a blank expression on her face. The same guy she saw push Michael up against the locker this morning. He had nicely done dreads but he was not her type.

"Are you talking to me?"

"Yeah. Who else would I be talking to? You see another person standing here?" Eugene asked.

"Oh I'm sorry, I'm Denise."

"Denise…. I'm EJ. I saw you and your people move across the street this weekend."

"Oh…okay…so you're one of my neighbors?"

"Yeah I know you goin' let me show you around. Introduce you to some people. Let me get to know you and you get to know me. You see that boy over there? Light skin, blue shirt, talking to that blonde?"

"The guy with the nice brush cut?" Denise asked.

"That's my homeboy. Name's Tremaine. Most of his friends call him Tre'. We can protect you and get you all the friends you need. As a matter of fact, we can come by and pick you up for the party tonight. We'll be there around seven."

Before she could decline, the dismissal bell rang and both Eugene and Tremaine were out the door.

How dare he? Denise thought as she pulled clothes out of her closet and dresser. He didn't even ask her if she wanted to go. He told her she was going! She would've cussed him out if he hadn't run off so fast. He must've thought she was another Michael. Well he had it all wrong! She would let him know that at the party tonight.

"What in the world?" Neicy Gray asked as she walked into her daughter's room. She knew something was wrong because there were clothes everywhere. "What is your problem?"

"Sorry, mom," Denise replied. "There's this party tonight, and I want to be flawless."

"What party? Where is it at? Are any parents going to be there? Did you ask Will?"

"A back-to-school party at some guy named Corey's house, and I'm sure his parents are going to be there considering the fact that the whole school and neighborhood knows about it. No, I didn't ask Will because I didn't think I had to."

"Yes you have to! He's the only reason we have a roof over our head and food on our table. I don't know how we would make it without him. Call and ask him now! He's at work."

"Alright....whatever." Denise rolled her eyes as her mom walked away. She remembered a time when her mom used to have a banging body and an independent attitude. That woman had disappeared and left a fragile, scared woman as soon as Will Gray had stepped in the picture two years ago. Denise really never cared for Will and his temper, and he felt the same about her and her "teenage mood swings."

"Hey Will", Denise said as he answered his cell phone. "There's this party tonight and everyone is going to be there. Mom said to ask you if it's okay for me to go."

"Sure, honey," Will replied between clenched teeth, "If it's fine with your mother then its fine with me." Not even giving her a chance to ask what her curfew was, he hung up. She could tell by the tone of his voice that he wasn't happy and trouble would definitely be waiting when she came home that night.

Chapter 3

"What in the world am I going to do for this project?" thought Michael. What was something he could create to describe himself? Maybe he should just turn in a blank paper- that described him very well. After all there was nothing interesting about him. He had no talents, friends, and to him it seemed like he had no life.

As his mom pulled up at the grocery store, he decided that he just wouldn't do the project or any of the other homework. "How about we have chicken, rice, and string beans for dinner?" his mom asked him, interrupting his thoughts.

"Huh....Oh yeah....I guess ma..." Michael replied, "I'll go get the drinks. What kind do you want?"

"That's a stupid question", said Jonathan, his eight year old brother. "What kind do I always drink?"

"Shut up Jonathan", Michael said as he walked away. Sometimes his brother could get on his nerves but other times he was an alright kid. Especially when Michael had chores he didn't feel like doing or if the remote control was on the other side of the room and he didn't feel like getting up to get it.

Today, though, he didn't want to be bothered by anyone. He needed his alone time.

As he left the isle with the soda and passed the alcohol isle, he spotted the jock that all the girls loved- Tremaine Webb. Tremaine didn't even glance in his direction. "If only I could be that guy", Michael thought. "If only everyone could love me, but then again what kind of world would that be? A crazy world- where fish walked and giraffes swam. A world that hadn't existed before and most likely would never exist in a million years.

When they got home, Michael and his brother started to take the grocery in the house, while his mom talked to a new neighbor from down the street. When they had taken in all the grocery, Michael had remembered that he hadn't closed the trunk and walked back to the car. He stopped in his tracks when he saw that his mom wasn't moving. She was just starring at the road and it was almost like she was in a trance. "Mom are you okay?" he asked her.

"Yeah honey I'm fine", she replied, "Are you not going to that party that all the kids are going to?"

He acted like he didn't even hear her and walked away. She knew he had never been to a party. He didn't even want to think about that party right now. Right now he was concerned about his mom. Even though she said she was fine he could tell something just wasn't right.

Later that night, she came in his room and told him Dorie and Nick London, Tremaine's aunt and uncle, were having a neighborhood block party on Saturday. She hadn't asked him if he wanted to go because there wasn't a need to. She would just go by herself. The woman never went out to clubs or for drinks with her friends. She had been single for as long as he could remember. The only man he thought his mom truly loved was God because if she wasn't at home or work, than she was definitely at church. She made him go at least 3 Sundays out of a month.

Personally, he didn't like it and he felt like his mom needed another man in her life other than Jesus. She had discussed neither his nor his brother's father. She just told him that both of their fathers were sorry drug dealers that walked out on her. They never bothered to give her one penny. Micheal never asked her more questions about his father and he never bothered to look for him. His mother always seemed like enough.

As a matter of fact he never wanted to have a relationship with any man. He felt like they were too much trouble to be around. He had never seen a good man in his whole life. Then again he didn't remember much about his life. He only remembered anything that happened since junior high. His elementary school years were a mystery to him.

The only memory he had about his early childhood was a picture his mom took of him when he was first born. He was the size of watermelon and as red as a tomato.

It was like there was a big gap between that first day and his first day at Jr. High School. It was like he had died and come back to life. Of course he sometimes wondered about what happened in that part of his life. He thought about asking his mom but she was always struggling and doing the best she could for them. He never wanted to stir up any trouble.

All of a sudden it was like a light bulb had come on and he knew what he was going to create for his project. Puzzle pieces that had to be put together in order for you to understand the real picture. The only problem would be that there would be missing pieces. Those missing pieces would be like the missing pieces in his life. Without those pieces you wouldn't understand the puzzle, just like no one (including himself), could understand him.

Chapter 4

Where are you going? Easter asked Eugene. "None of your damn business.....Stop being so nosey all the time!" he screamed.

Easter was Eugene's 16 year old sister that could be easily mistaken for a 21 year old woman. She had a Hallie Berry face, with Beyonce curves, and a Tyra Banks walk. As far as he knew she was still a virgin, but every boy in high school wanted to get with her (she always chose the nerds and losers though).

"Did you ask dad?"

"I don't have to ask dad a damn thing! If anything he needs to be asking me questions about what to do with his money after he sells all the shit loads of pot and weed he has! When he learns to come home every day and at least make sure we have food and are alive, then I will ask him what I can and can't do! Until then I'm the man of this house! Speaking of food....where did you get the money to buy dinner?

"A friend that's who!! Don't even ask who because it's none of YOUR damn business!! YOU need to stop being so nosey all the time!" She screamed even louder than him, as she walked in her room and slammed the door. It wasn't the first time they had argued and definitely wouldn't be the last! They argued all the time. Eugene thought maybe it was because they were so different. Whoever said opposites attract and likes repel was a lie! Then again they could be right because he was like an exact copy of his dad (which is not something he was proud of) and they didn't get along either. They barely communicated when the man decided to come home.

Eugene felt like his dad was a mean, nasty, selfish man, that was only smart when it came to selling drugs. He was the top drug dealer in town and somehow he had never gotten caught! Eugene admired how sly he was, but that was the only thing he admired about him! He hated that his dad left him and his sister to care for themselves. Some kids would probably love to have a parent like him. They probably complain about their parents being over protective, but he would kill to have a mother or father that at least fussed with him about being out past one in the morning! Most nights him and his sister had to go to bed hungry and either extremely cold or extremely hot depending on the season. Tonight, though, he wouldn't worry about his hunger or his body temperature. Alcohol, weed, and hoes would definitely fill him up.

"Did you get the drinks?" Eugene asked Tremaine as he climbed in the back of Tremaine's brand new car that he had just gotten from his aunt and uncle on his eighteenth birthday.

"Yea man don't worry about that. I got you!" Tremaine replied.

Eugene hadn't even bothered to speak to the three girls from the cheerleading squad that he seen in the back seat when he had gotten in the car. In his world hoes didn't deserve respect, they deserved to be used and put back whenever he felt like it! Tonight he didn't prefer the two in the back, his plan to get the new girl. She had a nice body. NO she had an almost perfect body!!! She could be his personal hoe because she was so easy to persuade. He knew before they even pulled up to her house that she would come running out to the car. When she did, he knew that she would do whatever she was told to do.

"Hey....Denise right???" Eugene asked as she got in the back seat beside the other girls.

"Yeah....."she replied.

"Well Denise this my boy Tre and Tre this Denise."

"Nice to meet you Denise", Tremaine said looking at her in the review mirror. "You look nice."

"Thanks!"

"What the hell is your problem?" Eugene asked her. "Relax! Loosen up! Damn!!!" He said. Then he reached in the back and grabbed the already spiked soda out the back and started pouring drinks. If she wasn't going to loosen up on her own maybe he should help her loosen up.

As someone opened the door to the brick, small, one story house, Eugene couldn't believe how packed the house was. There were people EVERYWHERE!! Right away he could see where the couples area was because people were in a small room tonguing each other down. Eugene made his way into the kitchen with Denise right by his side. She hadn't drunk more than two sips of the drink. It aggravated him that she just wouldn't relax! Bitch! He was already tired of her and they hadn't been together for more than 20 minutes. He decided to ditch her with his friend Jaden who was from out of town. Jaden could take care of her! He had other things to do that were way better than babysitting her!

Chapter 5

Well this was a little awkward, Denise thought to herself, sitting with a guy that she barely knew (well at least she knew his name, and that he was sexy!). Suddenly, Denise started to get butterflies. She had never had an attractive guy to actually like her, as a matter of fact most of the guys she had went out went in the past were far from it. It seemed like she only attracted losers. For once, though, a sexy guy had looked at her. Maybe this was it! Maybe, just maybe, he was the one for her.

As she looked up out of the daze she was in, she saw his hazel brown eyes staring at her. She was already in love with his light brown skin, Mohawk, diamond earring, and eyes. She smiled at him and he smiled back. It was cute, but awkward because neither of them said anything to each other. They just kept looking at each other like a fat kid looking at a freshly baked chocolate cake.

Luckily Tremaine came and broke the silence. "Jaden long time, no see man!!," he said. "What's been up with you?"

"Yea man it has been awhile.....you know me I just been chilling. What's been up? You still been trying to carry those boys to state?"

"You know it, we going this year!"

"Whatever man....Ya'll lucky y'all don't play us but I know a team that can beat y'all anyway!"

"Oh Really? Why don't we talk about while we go get you and the lady a drink?"

"Alright give me a minute....so your name's Denise huh?" Jaden asked her.

"Yes", she replied.

"Okay Denise I'm going to go get us some drinks. Can you hold my phone until I get back....I don't want it to fall out my pocket or make a mistake and lay it down somewhere."

"Sure", Denise said as she watched Jaden walk away with Tremaine. After they were out of her sight, she looked around and realized why she didn't come to parties- she didn't fit in the party crowd! Everyone here were like wild animals while she on the other hand was like a trained puppy. She would prefer sitting home and reading a book than being here. To pass time she played with Jaden's phone for a little while and even added her name to his contacts. After that she just got tired of sitting there!

She got up to leave and as she looked up she caught Jaden's eyes looking at her. She returned the stare and then walked out of the house quickly. As she reached the end of the driveway, she heard someone yell her name. Before she had even turned around, she knew it was him.

"Leaving early, aren't you? Are you taking my phone too?"

"Oh I'm sorry! I forgot I had even had it, here you go." She said embarrassed.

"So why you leaving so early? The party is just getting started!"

"Curfew..... got to be on time, you know?"

"Yea, well I can take you. Here is your drink.....let me just go grab my jacket!"

Before she could even say no thank you he had handed her the drink and he was already stepping in the house to get his jacket.

The ride home was just like how the night was so far- awkward! Plus she had started to feel a little funny. Jaden dropped one of his friends off home first. Then he dropped off some other girl that he gave a hug to after he walked her to her door step. Denise couldn't help but feel a little jealous even though they weren't dating. The girl had worn black wedges and a very short tight fitting red dress. She was pretty sure he was just dropping the girl off but after they hugged each other they walked into the house. Then they were gone for at least 20 minutes. She even dosed off because it seemed like everything was blurry.

Finally, he came out of the door and started the car to take her home. They still didn't talk much, they just kept exchanging glances. Well....they did talk about how to get to her house. When they arrived at her house, he turned off the engine and just stared at her. He told her not to worry about the dizziness she felt and said maybe she was just tired and she could go home with him but she declined. He opened the door and they gave each other a long, tight hug. When they were about to pull away, they looked into each other's eyes and kissed. It was a kiss like no other......it had a lot of passion behind it, yet they didn't have any feelings for each other...or did they? They couldn't......they barely knew each other!

They smiled at each other, and not saying a word, Denise walked away calmly and went in the house. A minute later, she heard him pull off. Until now, Denise hadn't ever believed that love at first sight was real......she thought it was just a saying. Now she knew it was a lot more than that. She walked unsteadily to the bedroom. She heard her mother scream but wasn't sure if it was just her imagination. The thought of Will on top of her mother or vice versa disturbed her and made her head hurt even worse. She decided to go to her room and made sure to lock the door before she passed out on the bed.

Chapter 6

"Tre, open this door right now!!!"

Why was she yelling first thing in the morning? Tremaine thought to himself, couldn't a man recover from his hangover in peace?!

"TREMAINE MARQUEZ WEBB... IF YOU DON'T OPEN THIS DOOR..!!!"

Tremaine heard her but he laid there for a few seconds. He remembered back to when he was around eight years old. His mama would tell him to come here or to do something for her and he would just continue to do whatever he was doing. She would say she was going to count to five and he would act like he didn't care but by the time the word "four" rolled off her tongue he was right there and did whatever she wanted quickly. One day after she got to two she didn't wait and he got the worst ass whopping of his life. He learned his lesson that day! Now he usually just came when he was called.

"Yeah ma, what's up?" he said sluggishly. She wasn't his biological mother, she was his aunt, but that's what he called her. His mother had died when he was fourteen. She was giving birth to his sister who also died as soon as she was born. He only remembered seeing his father once. That was the day when….he tried not to think of that day, but he had nightmares about it every night. He was in the fifth grade and had just gotten home from football practice. There was an unusual car parked in the drive way and his mother was not in the living room or the kitchen. He was about to go to her room when he heard her screaming and sobbing. He saw drops of blood as he walked up the stairs. His mother's bedroom door was locked, so he knocked. A few seconds later, the crying ceased to a whine. The door opened and a tall man appeared. There was a look in the man's eyes that Tremaine would never forget. The man told him that everything was fine, but he didn't believe him. He tried to push the door but the man aimed a gun through the crack and told him to wait in his room for his mother or he would kill both of them. The man also warned him not to call for help. He was terrified and went to his room. When his mother came to the room about 20 minutes later she explained that the man was his father and he just wanted to talk to her in private. After that incident, whenever he would come home and see the car in the driveway he would just walk to one of his boys house. In the eighth grade, he was shocked when he found out she was even giving birth. She never had said anything about being pregnant and you couldn't tell looking at her. She always seemed normal and happy. His aunt had rushed her to the hospital and he never saw her again except in his dreams when he heard her screams and tried to push the door to save her. His "father" did not show up at the funeral or try to be in his life. His aunt and uncle had taken care of him after their tragic loss. They were mom and pops to him.

"What's up? How about good morning?" she said.

"Sorry, good morning ma!"

"Thank you....did you know the neighborhood block party is going to be here today?"

"Man, I forgot!"

"Well now you know so let's get going!! We have a lot of cooking and cleaning to do, and you need to cut the grass, your uncle had to work."

"Alright man", he said grabbing his still throbbing head. This was going to be a long day!

The neighborhood block party…..something he hated but something his aunt always loved to do. They had finished cleaning up and he had cut the grass. His aunt had made a variety of food….fried chicken, baked mac-n-cheese, sandwiches, hotdogs, burgers, EVERYTHING YOU COULD NAME!!! People were starting to arrive and they brought even more food with them (mainly desserts). Black people never really bought much to cookouts except other people, but the best part about the whole thing were the pies and cake! He never could wait until everyone got there…he was always the first person to get a piece of strawberry cake! He went and got the first piece he seen.

All the smells were love, they over powered the smell of the freshly cut grass. As he began to indulge himself, he looked up to see Denise approaching with a cherry pie in her hand. As she put the pie on the table, he could tell something was very wrong with her. She seemed like she was in another world. She didn't even look up or wave and smile at him. He could tell she had on a lot of makeup. When she took a seat next to a loud radio, he decided to go over and talk to her.

"Tre, I know you not eating all the cake already man!" It was Eugene, and Tremaine knew it before he even turned around. Eugene never missed a chance to eat free food, that's why Eugene was at his house almost every day. He not only ate a lot of sweets, he ate a lot of everything, but never gained weight. Both of them were that way.

"Shut up nigga!" Tre replied, "I was trying to get to it before you got here!"

"Yea, whatever, let's just get some food and play 2K."

"Alright"

They filled up two plates of food and made their way to the house. When they were almost at the front door, they spotted the one person that barely went anywhere, except school, his house, and the store- Michael. He had on some black jeans and a blue sweater.

Tremaine already knew Eugene was going to harass him. "You can go ahead I'll be up in a minute, I need more cake," Eugene told him as he walked off. Tremaine felt sorry for the kid but he wasn't Superman, it wasn't his job to save everyone.

He went upstairs and started to get the video game ready. As he glanced out the window, he saw everyone having a good time except Michael who was being picked on by EJ and Denise who seemed to be too distracted by her phone to even talk to anyone. They both looked miserable.

Chapter 7

That smell…… A smell Michael hated with a passion but it was so familiar. It was like the smell of death. He had never met anyone who came to the doctor's office and didn't get put in the hospital and die in a matter of weeks or months. The way he saw it, if you had to go to the emergency room, you might as well write and sign your own will; especially their emergency room. It was the definition of SORRY.

Today, he decided to come to the doctor's office because he had been sick for a couple of months. He thought maybe it was just from stress. All the bullying had probably gotten to be too much for him, but he just came to make sure it wasn't anything serious like the flu. He told his mother but she said it was probably just a little cold. Since she wasn't going to make him an appointment, he had decided to take matters in his own hands. He had been to the doctor a few times for check-ups but his mom had been with him.

He waited in the waiting room with four other patients. He realized the second thing he hated about doctor offices, and hospitals too, was the long wait. It was already bad enough that you were most likely going to die, but having to die slowly made matters even worse.

Forty- five long minutes went by before he was called into the back. The cute, short, blonde nurse took his temperature, pulse, blood pressure, and last but not least- his weight! He hated getting weighed because he always seemed to be getting bigger and bigger. After his fourth visit, the doctor stopped giving him the "you're obese and need to go on a diet" talk. They probably realized there was no hope for him, he thought. When the scale stopped moving, he wasn't sure who was more shocked him or the nurse. Instead of weighing his normal 330 pounds, he weighed 319 pounds! For once, he had actually lost weight!

"Woooow", said the nurse, "when did you decide to start dieting?"

"Uh...I don't know", he replied.

"Well, I know Dr. Nelson will be very proud of you!, she exclaimed. " You can wait in this room right here", she said taking him down the hall to a room where he had to wait for the doctor. Luckily, the doctor came in five minutes later.

"Good afternoon Mr. Michael, where's your mother? You've never been here without here before."

"She told me to come on my own this time."

"Oh Okay," Dr. Nelson said shocked. "What's the problem?"

"Well I've been having this cold for months and I can't get rid of it! I think it's getting worse!"

"Have you been taking any medication?"

"No"

"Well I see you've lost weight...great job!"

"Yea...but I haven't been dieting."

"Oh"...Dr.Nelson said looking nervous.

"Dr.Nelson is there something you need to tell me? You're acting very suspicious!"

"I just don't think you need to be here without your mother."

"But I am old enough to be here without her..." He said not looking in the doctor's eyes.

"Well she must wanted you to know..."

"Wanted me to know what?"

"What she has been hiding from you all these years...why she was against you going to the doctor ever since you were born."

"Yea she told me it was time," he lied. " So tell me Doc...what's up?"

Nothing anyone said could've prepared him for what Dr.Nelson told him that his mom had been hiding from him.

Chapter 8

Denise applied more makeup to both her black eyes and decided to wear jeans and a shirt instead of a dress. This wasn't the first time Will had beaten her and then raped her afterwards. No...this was in fact one of many. Most of the time he did it for no reason at all. The only problem was that these last couple of times he hadn't been drunk at all, just angry. It was like everyday someone had pissed in his cereal- which she knew was impossible! Her mother would never do something like that!

She was more afraid of Will than anyone and it had been that way for as long as Denise could remember. Sometimes she hated her mom more than she hated Will because her mom let Will do those things to her and pretend that they didn't happen. She didn't know who her real father was, her mother never talked about him, but she hoped and prayed he was nothing like Will! They had to move to a different city all the time because of Will. Mom would say he got a promotion, but Denise knew he was fired because of his temper.

Tonight would be different than any other night, though. Tonight she wouldn't worry about Will, her mom, bruises, or black eyes. Tonight, she had her first official date with Jaden. She was excited, although she had to admit it was hard going out with a guy that lived out of town- a sexy guy at that! You never knew what they were doing or who they were with. In order to have the relationship that they had a person would have to have A LOT of trust. Denise lacked that trust, but Jaden's sexiness made up for it.

He was supposed to stop by and pick her up at seven. She went to let her mom know that she was leaving soon, when she heard her chatting with someone excitedly. She sounded the happiest Denise had ever heard her sound. When she entered the kitchen she saw Micheal's mom sitting at the island. Denise had forgotten that both their moms had been bonding a lot lately.

"Hey honey, you remember Ms. Drake?" her mom asked with biggest smile ever.

"Yes...I remember, hey Ms. Drake!"

"Hey honey, you look awfully pretty tonight! What are you up to tonight?"

"Oooo...um...going on a date.""

"With whom may I ask?"

"Um....a guy from out of town."

"Oh...ok...."Ms. Drake replied awkwardly.

"Well...honey are you sure it's safe?" her mom asked, " I mean...with the weather and all that being the way it is?"

"Well the weather was just fine when I came in", Ms.Drake commented.

Denise already knew her mom meant Will. "Yea mom, I'll be fine, she replied.

"Okay honey and Ms. Drake would like to ask you something..."

"Oh, I almost forgot! I heard you were an intelligent young lady and you know my son, Michael?"

Denise nodded.

"Well he's been having problems with his school work and I was wondering if you could tutor him? I'll pay you...I'm just so tired of seeing his grades look the way they do."

Not wanting to be harsh, Denise said yes, but when Ms. Drake started to ramble about her son she stopped listening. She heard a car horn.

"Okay, see you guys later," she said and ran out the front door. When she closed the front door, she left all of her problems behind her. Tonight was her night and it was going to be perfect!

~~~~~~
~~~~~~~~~~~~~~~~~~~~~~~~~~~

Perfect turned out not to be so perfect when Denise got into the passenger seat of Jaden's red 2010 expedition and seen two more couples in the back. She felt herself getting upset already!

Everything only seemed to get worse when they went to eat at McDonalds and he told her she had to eat off the dollar menu! After they got the food he barely talked to her. Then when they finished eating, Jaden and the 2 guys and one of their girlfriends went to the car to "talk". She and the other girl were left sitting at the table alone. Denise was like a boiling pot of water about to spill over! Just as she was about to get up and leave, she got a text message from Jaden:

Come to the car and bring Jasmine

When Denise got in the truck she saw the couple in the back feeling on each other like no one else was even there. They looked like they were really about to rip each other's clothes off!

"Where are we going?" Denise asked Jaden.

"Back to Steven's crib to Netflix and chill for a while."

Denise didn't reply, she just turned and looked out the window. She already knew what that meant. When they got there they were instructed by Steven's to go in the bathroom because the other couple wanted the bedroom and Steven had called the living room. Denise had gotten a little upset because she was hoping that they would really watch a movie, but it was obvious what everyone else came here to do.

When they went into the bathroom, Jaden started to tell her how beautiful she was and she wanted to believe it but she knew it was all just a bunch of bullshit. She opened the door to leave. "Don't come out here, I'm naked!" Steven yelled. Now she was stuck she thought. Jaden closed the door back and told her to relax and started kissing her. Yes, she wanted to do the big IT, but she wasn't ready and this didn't even feel right! She made him stop, opened the door, and sat on the sink to wait until Steven and his girlfriend were finished. Jaden sat on the edge of the tub angrily and played with his phone.

Minutes later they heard moans and groans all over the house. Suddenly, Jaden got upset. He closed the door forcefully and cut off the lights. "You're doing this, I don't care what you say!" he yelled at her. The next thing Denise knew she was on the sink with her panties at her ankles and him inside of her. Oddly, though, she didn't feel anything. She thought it was supposed to hurt like most people said. Maybe it didn't because she didn't want to do it. He made her have sex with him, but there was no need to scream because he was technically her boyfriend and she had put herself in the situation. She sat there listening to his groaning. Five minutes later Steven knocked at the door.

"Jay, ya'll got to go! My parents are on the way!" Steven yelled. They put on their clothes hurriedly and opened the door. Denise grabbed her phone off the counter.

"Go wait in the car", Jaden said and then he kissed her.

When Denise got in the car she looked at her phone to see what time it was and realized that she had Jaden's phone! Being curious she decided to go through it. She went through his pictures first and found naked pictures not just of one girl- there were so many that she couldn't even count them! She got so sick of looking at them that she decided to just go and give him his phone his phone back.

The front door to Steven's house was cracked. She looked through it and found Steven and Jaden paying the other guy. They had used all the girls and made some kind of a bet on them! Denise was so shocked that she just decided to get back in the car. This had been the worst night of her life! Not only had her first time been horrible, she had been part of a stupid bet!!

Chapter 9

"Mike, Mike, Mike........how much money you got for me today bruh?" Eugene asked as Michael as he pinned him to the locker.

"I only have two dollars but you can have it", Michael replied softly and passed him the wrinkled up money.

"Two dollars, That's all you got? What?! Your mama wont on her knees last night? Tell her to make sure she has more than that for me tomorrow, he said and walked away. He wasn't going to hit Michael today. He hadn't eaten in a couple of days, so he barely had the strength to ball his hand up into fist.

With two dollars he couldn't even buy himself an entire meal! How in the world was he going to get him and his sister dinner tonight with two dollars?

Well....she would just have to get herself something to eat tonight! He didn't have time to worry today! He just wanted to relax today! So, he would stop and get a burger after school, go home, and smoke all of his problems away.

Where is my shit? Eugene thought to himself. He had searched in every drawer, cabinet, even in every little hole. There weren't many places his weed could be in a house that was so small. He decided that he would have to do a trash can search! He would check all of the trash cans in the house. He would start with the kitchen, and then he would check the one in his father's room. He doubted his sister had taken them because she hated smoking, but he would check her trash too if he had to!

He walked into his father's room. The walls were painted a light brown, and it smelled just like good, old Mary Jane even though his father hadn't been home since forever (at least not when they had been there). Everything in his room had looked the same. A person would've thought no one lived in there because it was so clean. The room definitely didn't match who his father was. He went to the trash can beside the bed and didn't find anything, but as he looked up on the dresser, he saw something he had never seen before- a picture of his dad and another woman holding a smiling baby girl. He was sure the woman wasn't his mother (his father claimed his mother was a junkie who had left them and never came back) and he was also sure that the little girl wasn't his sister. His sister was a chubby baby, this baby on the other hand was small and looked friendlier. The baby kind of favored Denise but he knew that was impossible. He decided to figure it out another time. He had to find his weed! He had no other choice but to check his sister's trash can.

He opened the door to her messy, purple painted room. He went to the purple and white trash can and started to search through it. He didn't find the weed but what he did found shocked him a lot more than the weed would have! In the trash can was a pregnancy test with a plus sign on it.

A walk....that was just what he needed! A walk would clear his mind...no, a blunt would! A blunt after a walk would be even better!

He couldn't understand how his sister could let this happen when she knew they were already going through enough! He was definitely going to get to the bottom of all of this. He had tried to as soon as he had gotten over the shock of seeing the pregnancy test. He had called her and after she finished yelling at him about invading in her privacy, she told him the baby was by some guy at school, and he didn't have to worry because she was going to get rid of it. Even after hearing all of that, he felt like there was something that she wasn't telling him. He would figure it out after he smoked.

When he walked in to the corner store, Tremaine stopped him in his tracks. "Man if you're looking for some rillos they're all out but I can take you to the store on the other side of town."

"Damn, alright man....I might just need some of whatever you been drinking." Eugene told him, he could smell the alcohol on his breath and his eyes were bloodshot red(they got like that whenever he drank or smoke).

"Man...shut up and let's go!"Tremaine yelled for no apparent reason. Eugene got in the car. He knew Tremaine would always drink and drive, this wouldn't be the first time. He was the only person Eugene knew that never got caught doing it or never got in an accident!

Tremaine drove to the store that was on the other side of town. It was about 20 minutes away. When Tremaine pulled up to it, he didn't even realize he was at the back of the building, not the front where the store was, but Eugene didn't mind walking down the dark alley, he wasn't afraid.

As he walked down the alley he seen prostitutes lined up against the wall. Pimps, drug dealers, crack addicts, EVERYTHING! It looked like the pimp was giving the prostitutes some instructions. "Tonight, do whatever you have to do to get my money, you understand?" Eugene heard him say.

Eugene was walking pretty fast but after he heard that voice, he started to slow down. The voice sounded so familiar! "My favorite girl, have you done what daddy told you to do yet?"

"No sir, but I will have it done in a couple of days," A female's voice replied.

"That's good! No later than that, though, because when you waste time, you waste money and you know I don't play about my money!"

"Yes sir"

Eugene still couldn't figure out the male voice but he knew the female voice like he knew the back of his hand! It was his baby sister. It was Easter Norman. He took off running back to Tremaine's car.

They drove off to Tremaine's house where Tremaine went to sleep and Eugene stayed up thinking about what he had just witnessed.

Chapter 10

Tremaine woke up at 4 pm the next day with a major hangover. He barely remembered anything that had happened last night but he was sure Eugene would refresh his memory. Tremaine looked over at Eugene sitting in his blue recliner. Eugene looked like he had barely slept last night and even though his eyes were on the TV; it looked like his mind was in another world. "Are you alright EJ?" Tremaine asked him.

Eugene didn't respond. Tremaine was shocked; he had never seen Eugene like this before.

Just as he was about to ask Eugene what happened last night, his uncle came in the room. "Tre, can you go to the store with your aunt to make sure she doesn't spend all of my money. As a matter of fact can you go there for her as soon as possible? You know I don't like for ya'll to waste time, cause when you waste time you waste money, and you know I don't play about my money, you understand son?"

"Yes sir," Tremaine replied. When he closed the door, Tremaine looked back at Eugene. His blank look had turned into a murderous look. "Yo man, what is up with you?"

"Your....uncle....knocked...up....my....sister," Eugene said between clenched teeth.

"Man, what the hell are you talking about? My uncle is a minister at the church."

Eugene began to explain everything and after he was finished Tremaine didn't know what to believe.

"Take me back to that store tonight," Eugene told him, "and you will find out the truth."

On the ride back home from the store, Tremaine couldn't figure out how he was going to explain everything to his aunt. He told Eugene he needed to drop him off home until he got everything straight. He couldn't believe everything Eugene had said was true! Tremaine's uncle was a pimp and Eugene sister was one of his hoes and she was having his baby. His baby....and she was only 14 years old and he was a 41 year old man! His uncle could go to jail if the right person found out and the church would have a fit! He wasn't even aware that sex trafficking still existed.

Not only did they see his uncle and all his girls, they saw Jaden making out with some girl! Last night was just a crazy night!

When he opened the front door to his house and went in the living room, it looked as though he wouldn't have to explain much to his aunt. She looked depressed, shock, and upset, all at once.

"What's wrong Aunt Dorie?"

"Well I was upstairs talking to your Uncle Will about coming over tomorrow, when I heard a phone ringing in your pop's drawer. It was his phone.....a phone that I didn't even know he had! I picked it up and seen pictures and numbers of a lot of other women and the text messages they were ridiculous! I...I....I just can't believe it! Fifteen years....fifteen long years of being faithful and loving him and he did this to me!"

Tremaine decided to tell his aunt everything he knew. Watching her cry made his tears fall! After he told her everything he decided to leave and give her some alone time. He got in the car and drove to Denise's house. He knew that she to needed to know the truth about Jaden and a good friend needed to be there to comfort her.

Chapter 11

As Denise looked in the mirror she noticed the bags under her eyes from crying so hard last night. She had to admit she was tired of getting cheated on, lied to, and hurt. She wanted Jaden to treat her like the queen she was, not the queen's maid. Even before Tremaine told her what he'd seen, she tried to break up with him, but every time she looked at his face she couldn't! He was just too sexy for his own good!

Today was the day, though, that she would look him in the face and tell him she was done being with him. After she showered, got dressed, and put on her makeup, she heard him blow his horn. They were supposed to be going to the movies today, but she wasn't. Her plan was to go to the car, tell him it's over, and walk away, leaving him speechless. She had the butterflies as she walked to the truck. When she opened the door, she saw his gorgeous smile first, and then she looked into his hazel eyes. The next thing she knew, she was on her way to the movies.

She was so upset! The movie turned out not to be a trip to the theater, but a trip to his house to watch the game with him and his friends. As soon as she got there she wanted to go home and get back in bed. She already had to tutor Michael In a couple of hours. She decided to call Tremaine and ask for a favor.

It didn't take him long to come and pick her up and it wasn't hard for her to leave out the house unnoticed.

When she got in the car, she noticed he was staring at her. "What wrong with you?" she asked.

"Nothing, you're just the most beautiful girl I've ever seen!" Tremaine told her lovingly.

"Wow….really?"

"Well…yea…except for Beyonce," he said laughing.

"Why do guys think she is so beautiful anyway?"

"Maybe because she has beautiful physical characteristics and most guys don't look past that."

"Do you?" she asked him

"Well I would if I could," he laughed, "you can be a beautiful girl and have ugly characteristics which is a big turn off for me."

"Oh really?"

"Yea, what are some of your turn offs and turn ons?"

Their conversation continued like this until she had arrived home. Denise had to admit it was the best conversation and most fun she had ever had with a guy. She felt very comfortable around him....it was like she had known him for years!

"Thanks for the ride," she said.

"You're welcome. Anytime...that's what friends are for," he replied.

Her day had been like a roller coaster ride all day. It went down and then up and now it was about to go back down again because she had to tutor Michael, even though she really didn't want to.

He came around 5:30 and he looked upset and afraid. After going through some Spanish lessons first, she decided to ask him a question.

"Michael, why do you let people run over you?" she asked quizzically.

"Why do you?" he replied.

"What do you mean?"

"Well", he said nervously, "I always felt like victims were born with a sixth sense...they know when they are in the presence of another victim."

Denise just sat there shocked. Then as she looked down and up again she felt two large tear drops come from her eyes. For the first time ever, she didn't try to wipe the tears away, she let them flow, because across from her was someone who felt her pain and let their tears flow too. She already knew not only would she teach him, but he would teach her also. This was the beginning of another new friendship.

Chapter 12

Eight months later.......

Tremaine knew it was kind of corny but a two months after they became friends he showed up at Denise's doorstep with some flowers and asked her to go out with him. He was so shocked when she said yes and he had never been so happy!

Their relationship had started out very rocky, though, because Denise still hadn't broke up with Jaden and had major trust issues. Tremaine could understand that considering everything she had been through with him so he decided to give her some time. Not even a month later she broke up with Jaden because she started to fall for him even though she said she wasn't going to let herself. Their relationship started to get real but it was fun at the same time. Sometimes when they went out they even took Eugene and Micheal with them, but they never talked to each other. Eugene barely even talked lately, but Tremaine knew he was going thru a lot (he had just become an uncle after his sister had the baby prematurely). His sister had also fallen into a deep depression. He would always talk about finding bottles of pills in her room and all she did was sleep. Mental illness in the Black community was so devastating because people always choose to ignore it instead of get help. Tremaine prayed that everything would work out with for his boy's family.

Tonight, Tremaine was taking Denise out to eat some Chinese food, to the movies, and back to his place to meet his aunt. He was nervous and excited, but he was definitely more excited!

Dinner was good, the movie was better, and watching Denise become a nervous wreck when meeting his aunt was the best!

"Well I'm going to bed you guys, be good, and it was nice to finally meet you Denise!"

"Nice to meet you too," Denise replied as his aunt walked upstairs.

"Now was that so bad?" Tremaine asked as he cuddled up next to her on the couch.

"No...it was okay."

"I told you," he said. "I really appreciate you coming out with me tonight, you look beautiful."

"You always say that."

"You always do," he said and kissed her. One kiss turned into making out and making out turned into one of the best experiences he had ever had. It wasn't like any experience he had had with any other girl...It felt very different with every kiss and touch. He felt bad for having sex in his aunt's house while she was home but the moment was perfect. Maybe his aunt and uncle were getting a divorce but he had found the love of his life and he had lost his virginity to her.

"I have to get home or Will is going to kill me!" Denise said as she got up and fixed her clothes and hair. "Will Gray....he's my stepdad."

"Will Gray?", he asked.

"Yea...she replied, "do you know him or something?"

It couldn't be, he thought. "Well I have an uncle named Will Gray, he looks like this,

Tremaine said taking a picture out of his wallet and showing it to her.

"Oh my God.....it's Will!, she screamed.

"Uncle Will never told us he had gotten married! I have to go ask aunt Dorie about this!"

"No please...don't!", she begged.

Tremaine looked in her eyes and could tell she was terrified. "Why not?"

"Just please don't! Just promise that you will keep it between us!"

"Okay," he said, "let me take you home."

When he drove her home she was quiet the whole ride and she gave him an awkward hug when she got out. He was kind of depressed because he felt like maybe he didn't do as good of a job as he thought. When he was about to pull off, he saw a pair of angry eyes looking out the window and he knew they belonged to his Uncle Will.

Chapter 13

Michael was so excited as he looked at his report card and saw all B's and one A. He couldn't wait to tell Denise and his mom. Denise hadn't been in school the past couple of days so he decided to go by her house. The cars were there but no one answered the door when he knocked. He figured they were out of town or something and decided he would just tell her later.

He went home and walked hurriedly into the kitchen.

"Boy what's wrong with you?" his mother shouted.

"Look ma!" he exclaimed and handed her his report card. A smile spread across her face.

"Congratulations, son...I'm so proud of you!" She gave him a tight hug.

"Thanks."

"You know what? Tonight is going to be your night, we can do whatever you want to do!"

"Really?"

"Sure...you have any ideas?"

"Yeah," he said as his smile disappeared "Why didn't you ever tell me I was HIV positive?"

She didn't respond.

"You hid this from me all these years and thought I wouldn't find out? How did this happen and I want the truth!"

"Son, you don't need to know all of that!"

"I have a disease that's going to kill me and I don't need to know how I got it...Are you serious?!"

"Yes...leave it alone!" she yelled.

"No I'm not....it's my night, remember?

"Fine, sit down...I'll tell you the truth! When you were six years old, I met the most beautiful man I thought I'd ever seen. He loved me so much! He bought me anything I wanted or took me anywhere I wanted to go but whenever he made love to me he said he couldn't feel it. No matter what I did to try and satisfy him in bed, it didn't work! One day he got tired of me trying and said he was going to leave me. I begged him to stay and told him I would do anything he wanted. I didn't realize he was trying to set me up the whole time. He told me he would stay if I let him have you."

"Have me? What do you mean?"

"He wanted to have sex with you."

"Me? How? I was only six!"

"I know...but that's what he wanted and I told him I wasn't going to let that happen. He offered to pay me a thousand dollars and I needed the money...I had no other choice..."

"So you let him rape me?" he yelled and stood up.

"I'm so sorry son but you need to sit down...there's more..."

"Well, what can be worse than that?"

"For days and months after that you were hurt in every type of way and so was I. I went thru some of the man's mail and found out he was HIV positive. He came home drunk one night and confessed to it. I begin to panic! I just wanted you to be normal! I sent you outside to play and told you that you were allowed to ride your bike on the road. Just be careful I said and sent you outside. I took the man's car, because I didn't have one of my own, and drove around town for a while. I had a plan but I wasn't sure if I was going to go through with it. When I was driving up to the house, I saw you riding your bike down the street. I hit you, kept riding, and took the car and parked it a couple of minutes down the street. I came home and called the police, I told them I had found you outside and was sure you were involved in a hit and run. After that you were put in the hospital and I was told you would be unconscious for months and may suffer from memory loss when you awakened. Your skull had been fractured but had no other broken bones. After 5 months you woke up and didn't remember anything. I only helped you remember the good things about life like me and your brother. I home schooled you until I found a doctor that promised not to tell you about you having HIV and promised to do anything to help you. That's when I found Dr. Nelson and he was all the help I needed. He did everything he could all the time and he kept your condition a secret. There wasn't a flaw in my plan…. until now."

"Yea until now…I had to find out on my own and I would have never found out if I didn't get this stupid cold that keeps getting worse. You know what though? Whoever this guy is…I'm not mad at this guy…I'm more upset with you…What's his name anyway?"

"His name is Will…Will Gray."

"Will Gray? Denise's stepdad?"

She nodded. "Wow…"he said shocked. "You let this happen and tried to cover it up! You're supposed to love me? I hate you, he screamed and grabbed his jacket and left.

Chapter 14

"You stupid bitch!" Will yelled and hit her. "You never listen...you're a dumb whore! When I say come home, I mean come home! You're never allowed to go out of this house again...Do you understand me?" He didn't give her time to answer, he hit her again. "You want to make grown woman decisions huh? Come here! I'm going to treat you like a grown woman!" He dragged her to her room and threw her on the bed. The first time this had happened she yelled and screamed but after it had happened over and over again she had gotten used to it. She just laid there and waited for it to be over...she knew it wouldn't be long. Five minutes later he fell on her bed and went to sleep. ......

That's what had happened a couple of days ago...that was why she hadn't been to school. She couldn't leave because of coming home "too late" even though Will never gave her a curfew. She knew the beating and rape weren't really for being late, she figured Will was starting to discover that his nephew knew he had a second family. Denise didn't understand why Will was so ashamed of them. If anything they needed to be ashamed of him...he was the angry alcoholic! Denise didn't even want to see him today! She hated seeing him even days after a beating because he still gave her the same hard stare, not showing even a hint of pity.

Today she would stay in her room all day, like she had done the past couple of days. She wasn't allowed to talk on the phone to anybody or answer the door. When Michael came by she wanted desperately to scream for help but she was afraid of being heard by Will, and then being hurt by him more later. So, she watched him knock and walk away after not getting any answer. It seemed like today had been a long day but she looked and the clock and it was only 6. All of sudden she realized that she was starving! She knew all that was in the kitchen was mostly junk food, which she didn't eat much of, but she would eat almost anything at this point. When she got to the top step, she saw Will sitting at the bottom and heard Ms. Drake's voice talking to her mother. She could tell Will had been trying to eavesdrop just like she was.

"I have to tell you something about Will," Ms.Drake told mom.

"What about him?" mom asked.

Ms. Drake told mom everything about what had happened to her son and everything she knew about Will's condition and life.

"So Annette...you came here to tell me my husband's gay and is HIV positive?"

"Yes...I'm sorry I just felt like I needed to put the truth out there at least for my boy. I have had the condition for years and have just lost weight but I never got real sick, but he has."

"Annette, I don't believe you! Get out of my house!"

"But...it's the truth!"

"Get out!" mom yelled even louder.

As soon as Annette walked out the door, Will ran upstairs. Mom went up behind him and closed the door seconds later. It was the first time Denise had ever heard her mom yell at him. He didn't let it go on for long, Denise heard her when she hit the floor. She started to think about everything she heard Ms.Drake tell her mom. If it was true not only was she at risk but so was she, her mom, Tremaine, and there was no telling who else! So many questions were running through her head. How had Will gotten this disease? How long had he been gay and what made him want to be? Is this why he drank so much and was always angry? She couldn't even think of another question....a second later she couldn't even think. She had been hit on the back of the head and felt herself falling down the steps.

Chapter 15

Tremaine decided to tell his aunt about Uncle Will and the second family he had never told them about. Aunt Dorie was uncle Will's younger adopted sister and they had been very close since they grew up together. He didn't understand why Will hadn't told them. While they were talking they heard a knock at the door. His aunt went to answer it. "Well... we were just talking about you," she said.

"Where's Nick?" he asked quickly.

"He doesn't live here anymore."

"What...what do you mean?"

"Long story," Aunt Dorie sighed.

"Well sis I need your help and I need it fast!"

"Sure....what's wrong? I want the truth too....if you're not going to tell me that you don't want me help and have no reason to be here. Don't lie...you know I can tell when you do!"

"Alright...Tre go upstairs for a few minutes!," Uncle Will commanded.

Tremaine did as he was told but he didn't go all the way up the stairs, he stopped midway and listened.

"Well you don't know this but when we were younger, dad didn't go to work like he claimed he did when he left the house."

"Where did he go then?"

"He had another apartment that he went to just to sleep with other people."

"Women?" aunt Dorie asked.

"No...men...mostly little boys... I found out when I was thirteen. He took me there and told me he was going to teach me how to be a man and handle my business. He said you didn't need a woman- especially one that was easy to get knocked up and he said the experience was way better. He made me watch him at first and after a couple of times he wanted me try too, but I refused. He tied me down and made me. It was so weird...I figured anybody's first time would be though. When I was around 26 years old I met Annette Drake and she was so beautiful but I found myself more attracted to her son. The next thing I knew I was just like dad other than the fact that I liked women too. Some months later I found out I had AIDS and Annette found out too after I had raped her son. She made me leave and I was so depressed until a met this woman named Neicy Gray. The problem was she had a boyfriend named Eugene at the time. She didn't care, though; she went back and forth between me and him. They already had a daughter named Denise who I think Tre talks to now, that's why I didn't want him to hear this. Neicy left Eugene for me and we got married. It was okay at first but I just get upset because she can't satisfy me like a man can."

"Do you beat them?"

"Sometimes...but they're my property sis!!!"

"Uhm....and did I hear you say something about someone named Eugene?"

"Yea....he has a son and a daughter too I think and of course Denise."

"Oh...."said aunt Dorie.

"This time I went too far! I beat my wife too hard and I knocked her daughter downstairs but that was a mistake though! I had to tie both of them up and hide them in a secret spot! I'm scared that my wife may figure out a way to untie herself . She will never forgive me and will leave me! I can't afford that....I don't want to go to jail or see her with another man."

"So what do you plan to do Will?"

"Bury them...I guess."

"Okay...well then do it....without me...this is your mess so you clean it up!"

"What...you're not going to help your own brother?"

"No because my own brother already helped his own sister get HIV!"

"Dorie what the hell are you talking about?"

"My husband slept with Eugene's daughter. Thanks for the gift...now get out!" Will left out without saying a word.

Chapter 16

"Good Evening Ms.Drake.... is Michael here?"

"No son....I checked Michael into a hospital a few days ago. I was just on my way to see him...would you like to come?"

"Yea...sure"

"Alright let's go...what's your name son?"

"Oh I'm sorry...My name is Eugene...Eugene Norman."

~~~~~~

"Eugene....what are you doing here?" Michael asked with a confused expression.

"Nothing... I hadn't seen you in a while...just stopping by...."

"O well I guess you know why I'm in here...the full story and all... I know my mom told you on the way here."

"Actually, no, my sister told me when she found out my nephew was HIV positive and he had gotten it from her. I called Tremaine and he told me this long story about everything he knew.

I found out that you, and even me, are a part of the chain.

"Yea.....", Michael said sadly.

"Well, look man I just wanted to stop by and apologize for everything. You didn't deserve to be treated the way I have treated you."

"It's alright; at least it didn't kill me like this will."

"Well maybe not, you may out live me bruh! Congrats on your grades too man! Ready for graduation?"

"Yea...."

"Yea me too...I'll see you around man," Eugene said sadly and walked out of the door.

Chapter 17

Denise knew she had been hanging there for weeks beside her mother. She wasn't sure where they were at or how long they had been hanging there covered in bloody clothes. She was only sure of two things- that it was a bad storm outside and that they were going to die here. They just didn't know who was going to die first. Secretly, she hoped it was her because even though she didn't have a great relationship with her mom, she couldn't bear to watch her die.

"Denise, I'm so sorry...for everything," her mom said, "for putting you through this when I could've stopped it a long time ago. You would've been better off with your dad, Eugene. I love you so much."

Denise could hear her mother's voice but it was like she couldn't reply. She heard the footsteps approaching. She was pretty sure it was death because she could see her life flashing in front of her eyes.

To this day Michael hated thunderstorms or any type of storm for that matter. This wasn't even a thunderstorm...this was a tornado approaching. He looked up at the TV screen and saw the alert. He was going to stay calm, he didn't need to panic. He had already gotten extremely sick these past couple of weeks. So sick that he had to be put on a ventilator...that was pretty much the only thing keeping him alive. He had lost all of his faith .He listened to the sound of his breathing just to have something to concentrate on.

Seconds later the electricity went off. He knew this was it....He knew he was about to lose his life....

Who cared about life? Eugene thought. He sure as hell didn't...he was tired of it! Life was just too much! He was a poor brother, uncle, and friend with HIV. What was he needed for? Nobody needed him! He was tired...tired of trying to survive. He let the tears go and he made this best decision he felt he had ever made his whole life. As he jumped off the North Bay Bridge, he smiled. In a couple of seconds, all of his problems would vanish....

Vanish! That's what Tremaine needed his problems to do! He knew alcohol could help because it always did! He had been looking for Denise for weeks and couldn't find her...it drove him crazy! His Uncle Will had left town and wouldn't tell anyone where he had taken them.

He just wanted to talk to her and tell her everything and tell her he didn't care that they both may have AIDS! He would spend the rest of his life with her...they could die together! They wouldn't have any problems! She was just what he needed because alcohol wasn't helping. He had drunk so many drinks that he had lost count. It was a bad storm out and he couldn't feel the wheel under his hand. He couldn't even feel the car go off the road....

Epilogue

One week later……..

There were tears running down everyone's face all over the church. It was the worst funeral anyone had ever attended. Three friends walked hand in hand to the casket with tears falling down their faces. They had lost someone they would never forget…someone whose life wouldn't be the same without. Secretly, they wished it was them instead of the person lying in front of them. Why couldn't it have been? They all had problems of their own but they had all endured the struggle. Why couldn't their friend have endured it too? Their friend wouldn't get to get married, have children, or pursue their dreams. They wouldn't even be able to graduate next week.

More tears came down their faces as they saw their friend for the last time. They walked out of church wishing their friend could've made it to, but they had to face the reality that their friend didn't. For their friend it had been the last straw… It would be the last time anyone would ever see Denise White's face.

ABOUT THE AUTHOR

Student, poet, and author- JAUNKERRA SANDERS was raised in Plymouth, NC. She is currently a senior Psychology student at North Carolina Agricultural and Technical State University. The Last Straw is her first book, but she has written many poems since she the age of ten. The Last Straw highlights issues that many teenagers face worldwide. This includes things such as sex, sex trafficking, bullying, drugs, alcohol, and rape. In the future, she plans to be a teacher and school psychologist but will always continue doing what she loves the most-writing.

www.ingramcontent.com/pod-product-compliance
Lightning Source LLC
Chambersburg PA
CBHW031857170626
46807CB00004B/1779